# Nicholas
## and the Wild Ones

To the Little Boy I once was

JANETTA OTTER-BARRY BOOKS

Text and illustrations copyright © Niki Daly 2016

First published in the USA in 2016 by Frances Lincoln Children's Books,
an imprint of Quarto Inc.,
276 Fifth Avenue, Suite 206, New York, NY 10001
www.franceslincoln.com

ISBN 978-1-84780-853-0

Illustrated with digital art
Set in Mr Dodo

1 3 5 7 9 8 6 4 2

Printed in Shenzhen, Guangdong, China

# Nicholas
## and the Wild Ones

## Niki Daly

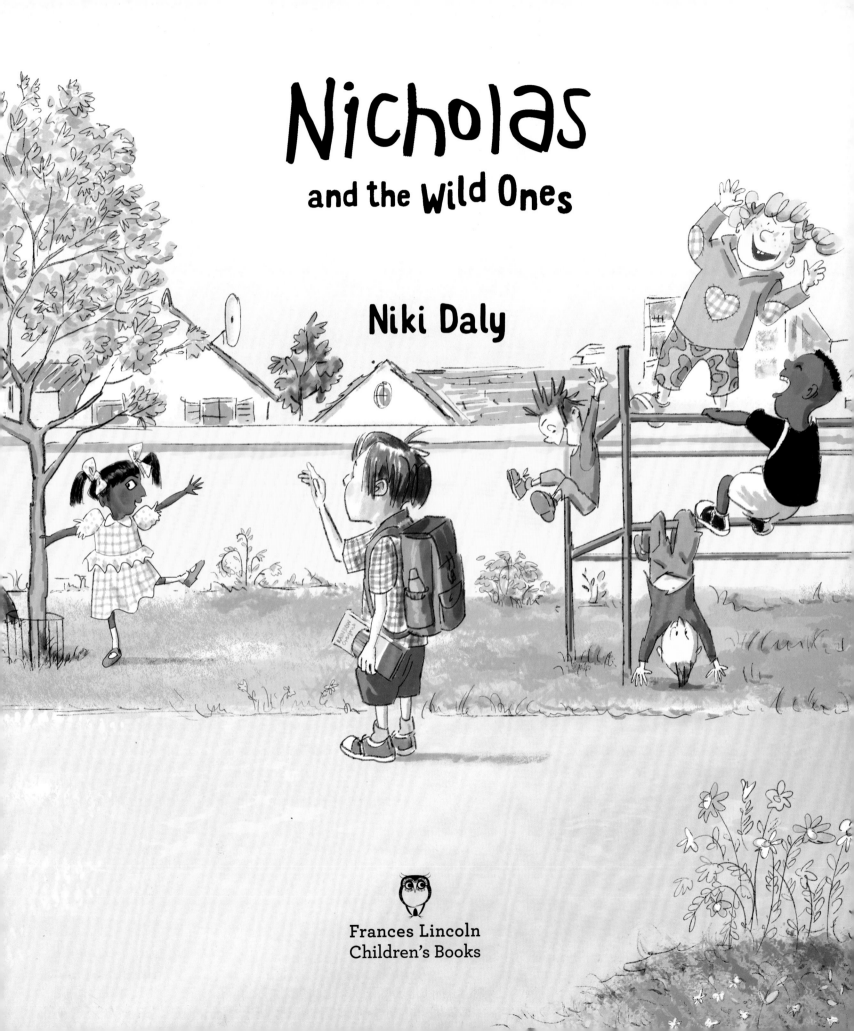

Frances Lincoln
Children's Books

**When Nicholas** came out of school,
Mom was waiting.

"How did you like it?" asked Mom.
"Not one bit," replied Nicholas.
"Oh dear, why not?" asked Mom.

"See those kids over there?" said Nicholas.
"Yes," said Mom.
"Well, those are the Wild Ones," said Nicholas.

Going home, Nicholas told
Mom all about the Wild Ones.
   "Charlie's the wildest," explained Nicholas.
"He stands on top of the climber and jumps
on anyone who passes below him."
   "That's dangerous," said Mom.
   "**Lethal!**" said Nicholas. "But you know who's really creepy?"
   "Tell me," said Mom.

"Wedgie Reggie," said Nicholas.
"He thinks it's very funny to yank kids
up by their underpants.
And you know what?"

"What?" asked Mom.
"My friend Stephen had to walk
around with his underpants
up his bottom."
"That's not very funny," said Mom.

"It's **mean**," said Nicholas. "But Big-Mouth Jake's even worse."
"Why?" asked Mom.

"At recess, he snatched Shakira's snack and stuffed it in his mouth. He didn't even close his mouth. You could see the goo going around and around like cement in a cement mixer."

"Gross," said Mom.
"**Mega gross,**" said Nicholas.

"But now I'm going to tell you about the
SCARIEST, WILDEST ONE IN THE ENTIRE WORLD!"
"Who's that?" asked Mom.

"Cindy Crocker.
She's as **big as a wrestler.**

She pushed me from behind while I was
showing Shakira my poop-powered
motor-car invention," said Nicholas.

"That's bullying," said Mom. "Did you tell Miss Pinkerton?"
"Yes," said Nicholas. "And you know what she did?"
"What?" asked Mom.

"After recess she read us a book about our rights. And NOBODY has the right to be horrid to us," said Nicholas.

"Quite right," said Mom.

"So, I won't be going to school anymore," said Nicholas.

When Dad heard about the Wild Ones, he said, "You've got to show them that you're not afraid."

"How?" asked Nicholas.

"By putting up your fists like SO," said Gramps.

"No, no," said Grandma. "Nicholas is an "ideas man." He'll think of a creative way to handle those Wild Ones."

"Yes," said Mom. "I'm sure you'll come up with a plan. But you've got to go to school. Otherwise, how will you become a famous inventor?"

So the next day Nicholas went to school—

and the Wild Ones were waiting for him.

Nicholas showed them he was not afraid
and put up his fists like SO!
This made the Wild Ones fall about with laughter.

So in art class, when Miss Pinkerton asked them all to draw something from their imagination, Nicholas drew a *Wild Ones Munching Machine.*

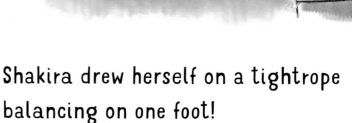

Shakira drew herself on a tightrope balancing on one foot!

Cindy Crocker drew a wobbly heart and colored it pink. The rest of the Wild Ones didn't know what to draw. Instead, they laughed at Cindy's pink wobbly heart, which made big tears plop out of her eyes.

"Cindy, dear," said Miss Pinkerton, "come and sit next to Nicholas."
"That's a cool pink wobbly heart," said Nicholas.

Miss Pinkerton was happy to see Cindy and Nicholas talking to each other at last.

# Uh-oh!

At break, Charlie jumped on Nicholas . . .

Reggie gave him a savage wedgie . . .

Big-Mouth Jake ran away with his packet of Space Snacks . . .

Then Cindy Crocker cornered him in the toy room and . . .

this is what she said.

"Can I come and play at your house?"

"Sure," said Nicholas.

After school, Mom was pleased
to see that Nicholas had made
a new friend.

"This is Cindy Crocker," he said
to Mom.

"This is my mom," he said
to Cindy Crocker.

That afternoon they had a really fun time.

Cindy showed Nicholas how to do a powerslam.

And Nicholas demonstrated his latest
solar-powered helicopter design in flight.

When the rest of the Wild Ones
heard about Nicholas's
cool helicopter design
they all wanted one.

So in art class he showed them
how to make their own.

And **that** meant . . .

Charlie didn't jump on anyone,

Reggie cut out
the wedgies,

Big-Mouth Jake
didn't even think
of treats.

Cindy thought of giving
Shakira a push, but didn't,

and **this** meant . . .

Shakira could show Nicholas how to balance
on one leg and make his eyes go like SO,

and Nicholas could show Shakira
how to hold her fists like SO.
Just in case the Wild Ones
ever turned wild again,
which they hardly ever did . . .

except some days, when they simply
HAD to be wild!

And that gave
Nicholas a new
idea . . .